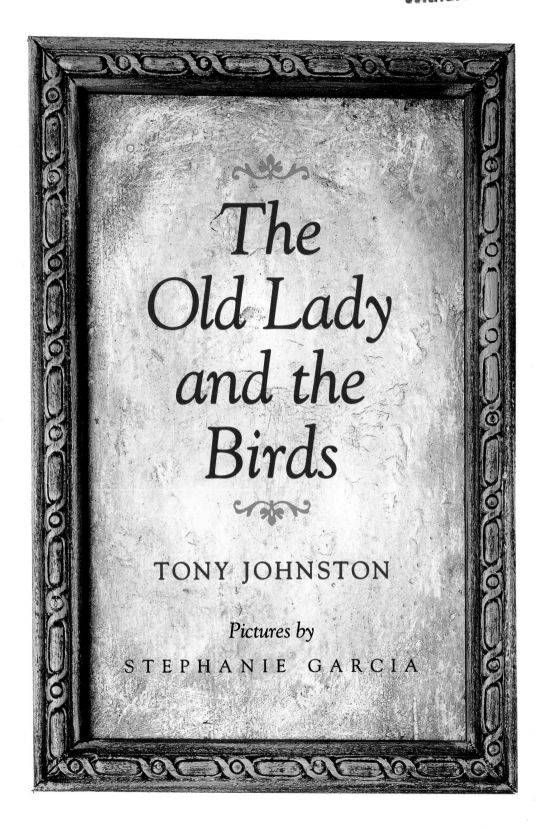

The Old Lady and the Birds

TONY JOHNSTON

Pictures by

STEPHANIE GARCIA

Harcourt Brace & Company

SAN DIEGO   NEW YORK   LONDON

Text copyright © 1994 by Tony Johnston
Illustrations copyright © 1994 by Stephanie Garcia

Requests for permission to make copies of
any part of the work should be mailed to:
Permissions Department,
Harcourt Brace & Company,
8th Floor, Orlando, Florida 32887.

Library of Congress Cataloging-in-Publication Data
Johnston, Tony.
The old lady and the birds/by Tony Johnston;
illustrated by Stephanie Garcia.
p. cm.
Summary: In her garden in Mexico,
an old lady enjoys watching the birds
and warning the cat to leave them alone.
ISBN 0-15-257769-6
[1. Birds—Fiction. 2. Gardens—Fiction.
3. Cats—Fiction. 4. Mexico—Fiction.]
I. Garcia, Stephanie, ill. II. Title.
PZ7.J647801 1994
[E]—dc20   91-45124

First edition
A B C D E

Printed in Singapore

For Allyn Johnston,
my dear editor,
who loves *los pajaritos*

—T. J.

For Mom, Dad, and David

—S. G.

THE OLD LADY
sits in her garden in Mexico
under the pepper tree
to watch the birds.

She breakfasts on fresh *bolillos*.
The birds hop onto the bread basket
to see what she is eating.
They steal bits of *bolillo*.

"¡*Ladroncillos!*" says the old lady.
"Little thieves!"

Leaves fall down from the pepper tree
like little green feathers.
The old lady sweeps them up.
The birds steal bits of broom
for their nests.

"*¡Ladroncillos!*" she says.

The old lady sews in the garden.
The birds steal bits of colored ribbon
for their nests.

"*¡Ladroncillos!*" she says.

When the birds bathe in the fountain,
they shake off water in little shivers.
The old lady puts up her parasol
to watch them.

She lunches on coffee and tortillas
in the blue afternoon.
"*¿Crema?*" she asks the birds. "Cream?"
"*¿Azucar?*" she asks as she stirs
the sugar round and round
till it dissolves in her cup.

But the birds want only tortillas.
So she tosses them bits
and sips the sweet coffee herself.

A cat steps out of the tall grass.
It likes the birds, too.

"*Deja los pajaritos en paz,*" she tells it.
"Leave the birds alone."

She gives the cat
a bowl of milk.

The sun is high.
The birds are singing.
The fountain is singing.
Even the cat is singing
in the sun.
The old lady smiles at that.

Later, like a little singing wind,
she drifts through the garden
to smell the flowers.
Slowly, so as not to scare the birds.

The cat stretches
and dissolves into the flowers.
It is not looking for coffee.
It is not looking for tortillas.

"Leave the birds alone," says the old lady.
"*Deja los pajaritos en paz.*"

The old lady scatters seeds
along the garden path.
She pours some into her lap.
Soon she sleeps in the sun.

The birds steal seeds from her lap.
She wakes and says, "*¡Ladroncillos!*"

Night folds its wings.
The moon rises white
behind the pepper tree
like a big bowl of milk.

The old lady closes her eyes
to hear the good-night song
of the birds
and the good-night song
of the cat.
She smiles at that.

Then she sleeps
till the moon dissolves
in the morning sky.
Till the sun comes up
and the cat wakes up
and the birds wake up
and begin to sing.

The original art in this book was created from various
materials including wood, Fome-Cor, modeling paste,
acrylic paint, clay, foil, wire, cloth, and dried flowers.
The text and display type were set in
Goudy Oldstyle and Goudy Oldstyle Italic.
Composition by Harcourt Brace & Company
Photocomposition Center, San Diego, California
Color separations were made by Bright Arts, Ltd., Singapore.
Printed and bound by Tien Wah Press, Singapore
Production supervision by
Warren Wallerstein and Cheryl Kennedy
Designed by Michael Farmer